WHY, OH WHY, AM I A CROCODILE?

WHY, OH WHY, AM I A CROCODILE?

For Gus, Lola & Teddy

Written by
ALEX BROOKS

Illustrated by
HANNAH WORSLEY

BIG TEETH

On the bank of a river,
beneath a palm tree,
Stood a tearful Crocodile,
as lonely as can be.

Staring in the mirror,
feeling hideously vile,
She cried, "Why, oh why,
am I a crocodile?"

Later on that morning, whilst out walking,
She looked up as she heard a squawking.

It was a beautiful parrot in glorious flight,
Broad wings dazzling and feathers bright.

Admiring the parrot for a little while,
She sighed, "**WHY, OH WHY, AM I A CROCODILE?**"

On she went, plodding miserably,
Then paused at the sound of a rustling tree.

There was an elegant giraffe, striding with grace,
With the longest lashes and the prettiest face.

Fascinated by legs that stretched a mile,
She groaned, **"WHY, OH WHY, AM I A CROCODILE?"**

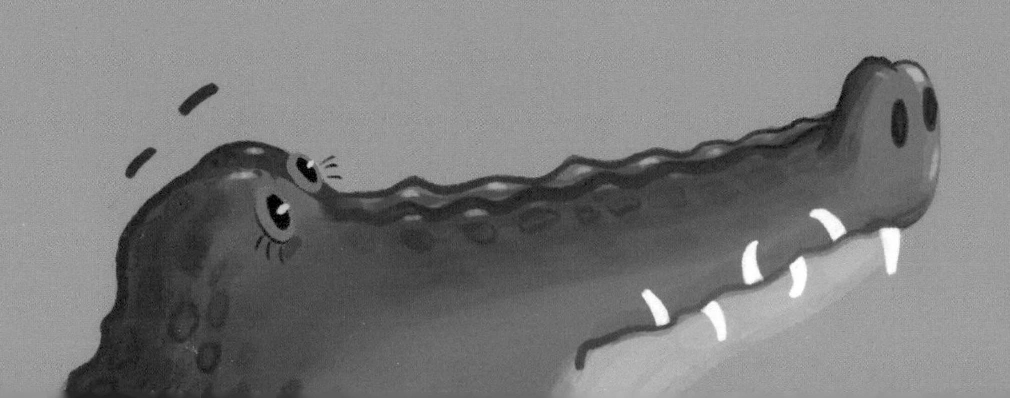

Then a lion appeared, with the loudest of roars,
Majestic body and enormous great paws.
Amazed by his teeth and perfect white smile,
She snapped, "WHY, OH WHY, AM I A CROCODILE?"

Deciding to take a stroll by the lake,
She spotted the most magnificent snake.
Stunned by his slithering, swanky style,
She sobbed, **"WHY, OH WHY, AM I A CROCODILE?"**

"WHATEVER'S THE MATTER?"

said a voice from a tree,
Crocodile looked up to see a swinging monkey.

She dried her eyes, blew her snout,
Then poor old Crocodile blurted out...

MY TEETH ARE
CROOKED
MY
EYES
ARE
SMALL
MY LEGS
ARE SHORT

MY SKIN IS LEATHERY,
HORRIBLE TO TOUCH

AND I'M FAR FROM TALL

AND AS FOR MY COLOUR,
WELL, I CAN'T SAY MUCH

MY BODY'S
FAT

MY TAIL'S TOO L O N G . . .

SO BASICALLY I'M JUST
ALL WRONG

Then suddenly with a crash and a thud,
There lay Monkey in a splodge of mud.

"Are you okay?" asked Crocodile,
"I'm fantastic!" he replied, with a smile.

"Well, apart from the fact I just fell from a tree,
But being blind has never stopped me...

I'm an adrenaline monkey, living life on the edge
(With the occasional somersault into a hedge!)."

Crocodile quizzed, "But you don't complain?"
Monkey replied, "Please let me explain...

I may be blind, but I am well,
I can hear, touch, taste and smell.

Accept yourself for who you are,
Take my advice and you'll go far.

There's really no need to feel sorry for me,
Instead, let's join my new friends for tea.

You see, I've met four others today,
Who are all feeling in a similar way,

A PARROT SO COLOURFUL
SHE JUST CAN'T BLEND IN,
TALL GRL2
A GIRAFFE THAT HATES
BEING TALL AND THIN.

A LION THAT WISHES
HE WASN'T SO SCARY,

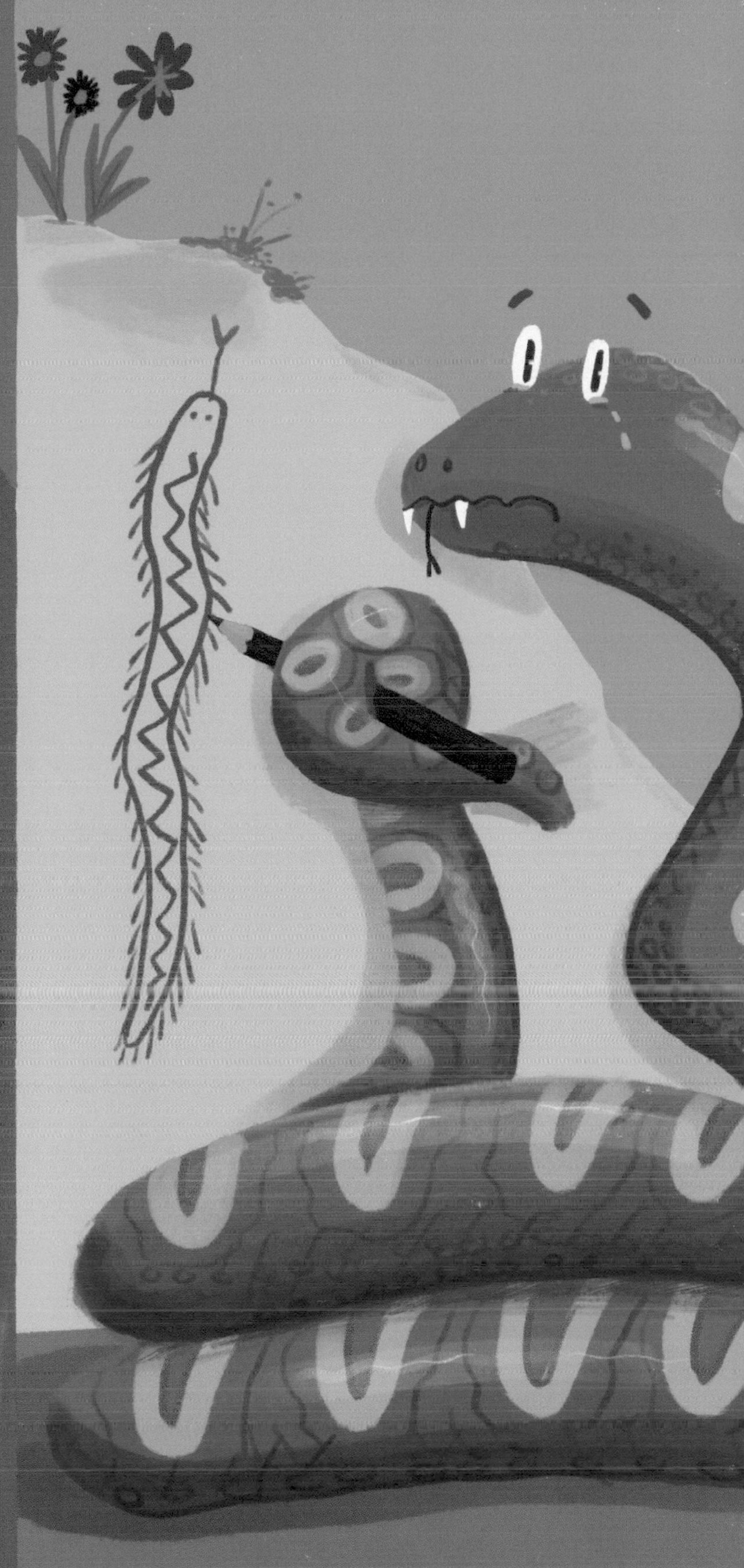

AND A SNAKE THAT DESPERATELY
WANTS TO BE HAIRY."

So as they drank tea and ate delicious cake,
They realised the difference talking could make.

It was clear now to Croc that they all felt bad,
But with help from each other, were no longer sad.

From that day forward, the new friends declared,
The best type of problem is one halved and shared.